Curly Carly

By Jenny Jinks

Illustrated by
Hannah Mccaffery

Chapter 1

Carly had very curly hair. She had always had curly hair, even when she was born. No matter how her mum tried to tame them, Carly's curls just bounced back. They were out of control.

But Carly loved her hair. That's because she had a secret: Carly's curls were magic.

She didn't know how, or why, but whenever danger or mischief was about, Carly's curls went extra, super-duper curly.

Carly's class was going on a school trip to
an ancient castle. All the way there, Carly's
hair was curling like mad. That was because
of Naughty Norman. He sat at the back of
the bus, playing tricks on people. Carly's hair
always went super curly whenever Norman was
around.

As the class walked up to the castle, a short,
grumpy man pushed past them down the steps.
He slammed the door of his fancy car and sped
away.

Miss Mills, their guide, was waiting for them at
the top of the steps.

"Sorry about him," Miss Mills told the class. "That's Mr Temple, the manager here. He's just found out the castle needs urgent repairs. It's going to cost a small fortune to fix."

"He thinks he's got it bad," said the security guard walking past. "We've all had to take a pay cut."

"Well I would happily work here for free," Miss Mills said, smiling. "I just love old buildings and all their history!"

Miss Mills showed the class inside, past two
suits of armour standing guard at the doors.

"You will notice lots of suits of armour all
around the castle," Miss Mills said. "They are
meant to keep unwanted people out."

"I can see why," muttered Norman. "They're creepy."

"Some say they're haunted," Miss Mills continued. "Apparently they have been known to move about on their own."

Chapter 2

Miss Mills took the class upstairs first. They looked around the lavish bedrooms, and walked across the battlements. Then they went down to the banquet room.

Miss Mills was right: suits of armour stood outside most of the rooms. Carly walked up to one. She could see why people thought they were haunted. She definitely felt like this one was watching her. Carly noticed her hair had gone extra curly again.

She peered into the banquet hall to check what Norman was up to, but he was talking to Miss Mills about the fancy gold candlesticks on the table. Carly would have to keep an eye on him.

"It's time for a break, but there's still plenty more to see this afternoon!" Miss Mills told everyone as she led them back out to have their lunch.

"That's odd," Carly said as they left the banquet hall. "I'm sure this suit of armour was facing the other way before."

"Maybe they're haunted after all," Miss Mills said, winking at Carly.

'Maybe,' thought Carly. Except she didn't believe in ghosts.

Chapter 3

After lunch, Miss Mills took them all downstairs.

"This is where the castle keeps all its secrets," Miss Mills told them. "From hiding places, to dumb waiters and secret passageways."

"A dumb waiter?" sniggered Norman. "That's a bit rude."

"It's not a person. It's a hidden lift that goes straight from the dining room down to the

servants' area," Miss Mills explained. She pointed to a small hatch in the wall. "People used it to transport and hide all sorts of things."

"Cool!" Norman said.

Carly's hair went all curly again.

What was Norman up to? Or maybe it was all this talk about secrets. But Carly didn't think so. Something strange was going on, and Carly wanted to find out what. Then Carly spotted something odd. There were fresh scuff marks on the floor next to one of the walls.

"Do people still use the dumb waiter and secret passageways now?" Carly asked.

"Oh no, they will all have been blocked up a long time ago," Miss Mills said. Suddenly Miss Mills's phone buzzed. "I'm sorry, there's something I have to deal with. Keep looking round. Just come back up to the entrance hall when you're finished." And she rushed off up the stairs.

Carly couldn't help but wonder what that was all about. She was sure it was important. Carly waited until nobody was looking, then she crept back up the stairs after Miss Mills.

"What do you mean they're missing?" Miss Mills was saying to the guard. Carly listened in from her hiding spot. "Who could have taken them?"

"I've been on watch all day. Nobody's been here except you and those kids," the guard said. "I've called the police. Nobody is allowed to leave until they get here."

"You can't possibly suspect the children of stealing golden candlesticks?"

"Who else could it be?" said the security guard.

"I suppose one boy was quite interested in the candlesticks, but…"

"I'm sure the police will be very interested in talking to him," the guard said.

Carly gasped. Not Naughty Norman. He might be cheeky, but she was sure he wouldn't steal. None of her classmates would. But that only left Miss Mills, and she seemed so nice. Something else was going on here, and Carly had to find out what, and quickly.

Chapter 4

Carly snuck back downstairs. She had an idea about how the real thief might have got into the castle, she just needed to test her theory. But, as soon as she got back downstairs, Miss Mills appeared.

"I'm afraid you're all going to have to come back upstairs," she said, looking very serious. "There has been an incident, and we need to talk to you all."

The class filed up the stairs. Carly hung back just long enough to give the wall a quick shove. It moved a tiny bit, scraping the floor.

'Aha!' thought Carly. Now she knew how they had got in, she just needed to work out who.

The police were already there when Carly reached the top of the steps.

"I am Detective Bridges," said a woman. "And I have to ask you all some questions about some items that have gone missing here today."

There was a chorus of gasps from the class.

"Well we didn't do it!" Norman said.

"Nobody is being accused of anything,"
Detective Bridges said. "We just want to talk to
anyone who might have seen anything."

Carly couldn't let them accuse Norman. She
needed to solve the case, and soon.

Suddenly Mr Temple's car came screeching up
the drive.

"What's going on?" he said, storming towards them. Carly's hair went crazy the second he walked past. She had a really bad feeling about him.

"I'm afraid some items have gone missing," Detective Bridges explained.

"Oh. Well, not to worry. I'm sure they'll turn up," he said quickly. Carly noticed him brushing some thick dust off the sleeve of his fancy suit.

Where had he been all day, she wondered, and why wasn't he more upset about the robbery?

"Well if you'll excuse me, I can't just stand around worrying about some silly candlesticks.

I've got work to do."

Carly gasped. Detective Bridges hadn't mentioned candlesticks. Suddenly, everything made sense.

"It was you!" Carly cried.

Chapter 5

"Don't be ridiculous," Mr Temple snapped.

"Why would I do a thing like that?"

"You need money. The guard said everyone has had to take a pay cut because of the repairs," Carly said triumphantly.

"But he left first thing this morning," Miss Mills looked confused.

"That's right, and I would have seen if he'd come back," the security guard added.

Carly had already worked that out.

"He used the secret passage to sneak back in," Carly explained. "Then he hid in the suit of armour until the coast was clear."

'That's why my hair went curly when I was stood next to it earlier,' she thought. 'He must have been hidden inside so nobody would see him! I knew that thing was watching me.'

"Search me. Search my car," Mr Temple snarled. "You won't find them."

Carly thought quickly. He wouldn't risk getting caught with the candlesticks. He must have left them somewhere safe where he could collect them later once the dust had settled... Dust! That was it!

"I know where the candlesticks are!" Carly cried.

She led everyone into the banquet hall and over to the dumb waiter. Miss Mills had said that nobody had used it for years. It was one of the only places in the castle that would be thick with dust.

Carly threw open the hatch. Sure enough, there were the missing golden candlesticks. Mr Temple looked extremely cross as Detective Bridges put him in handcuffs.

Detective Bridges shook Carly's hand. "Thank you for your help," she said. "We might never have caught him it wasn't for you. But how did you work it all out?"

"Oh, I had a little help," Carly smiled, tucking a curl behind her ear.

Detective Bridges laughed, and her own tight curls bobbed around her face. "I love your hair," Detective Bridges said. "Curls are just magic, aren't they?" and she winked at Carly.

Carly stared after her in amazement. Was it possible that Detective Bridges had magic curls too?

The End

Book Bands for Guided Reading

The Institute of Education book banding system is a scale of colours that reflects the various levels of reading difficulty. The bands are assigned by taking into account the content, the language style, the layout and phonics. Word, phrase and sentence level work is also taken into consideration.

Maverick Early Readers are a bright, attractive range of books covering the pink to white bands. All of these books have been book banded for guided reading to the industry standard and edited by a leading educational consultant.

Pink

Red

Yellow

Blue

Green

Orange

Turquoise

Purple

Gold

White

To view the whole Maverick Readers scheme, visit our website at www.maverickearlyreaders.com

Or scan the QR code above to view our scheme instantly!